D0475141

Reading Grows

Ellen B. Senisi

For Steven, with love. Still reading, still growing…

Also by Ellen B. Senisi: *For My Family, Love, Allie*

Library of Congress Cataloging-in-Publication Data
Senisi, Ellen B.
Reading grows / by Ellen B. Senisi.
p. cm.
Summary: Photographs and simple text provide an introduction
to the early stages of reading. Includes information for parents and caregivers.
ISBN 0-8075-6898-8
1. Reading (Early childhood)—Pictorial works—Juvenile literature.
[1. Reading.] I. Title.   LB1139.5.R43S46 1999   372.41—dc21   98-35245   CIP   AC

Text and photographs copyright © 1999 by Ellen B. Senisi.
Published in 1999 by Albert Whitman & Company, 6340 Oakton Street, Morton Grove, Illinois 60053-2723.
Published simultaneously in Canada by General Publishing, Limited, Toronto. All rights reserved.
Printed in the United States of America.
10   9   8   7   6   5   4   3   2   1

Reading Grows

Ellen B. Senisi

Albert Whitman & Company

Morton Grove, Illinois

Reading grows—bit by bit,

Baby reads with mommy.

Baby reads by herself, just like daddy.

/ Baby reads with mommy.

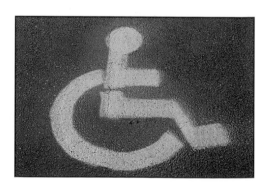

picture by picture.

"I can read anywhere!"

Reading grows—color by color,

Blue, yellow, red, orange, purple, green—what's your favorite color?

shape by shape,

Rectangle, diamond, triangle, square, circle, oval– what's your favorite shape?

story by story.

"When we're done, please read it again. And don't skip any words this time."

"This is my favorite part!"

Reading grows—letter by letter,

"I know every letter in my name!"

word by word,

On Monday, Red Mouse went first to find out.

cookie ran into the closet before the door close

sentence by sentence.

"Now let's read together."

Reading grows—book by book,

"Why aren't you listening to me?"

"I'm reading!"

"Why?"

"I have to know what happens next!"

by book,

by book,

and before you know it,

you enter the world of books.

You learn

what you always wanted to know.

You read stories, you write your own stories,

and you can help someone else learn to read.

Reading grows—just like you!

Reading grows, just as children do, and the process takes a very long time. Your children will begin their formal reading education in school, but that's not where they will really start to master reading skills. They begin piling up the building blocks of the reading process at home, from the time they are babies.

It can be hard for parents to find the patience and time to read with their kids—day after day, month after month, year after year. But finding that time and patience pays off. Everything parents want for their children's future is possible if the children become good readers. Educators disagree on many issues, but virtually all agree that daily reading is the most important educational preparation parents can give their children.

So help your child jump into reading at whatever level he or she is now.

The beginning years

From the time your children are born, read aloud board books or very simple picture books. Children will quickly learn what a book is all about—how the pages turn, how interesting words and pictures can be. They will enjoy the reading experience and look forward to it.

Read briefly but several times a day. You are establishing a lifelong habit for your child.

Help your young children to identify shapes and colors in books, on signs, and all around them. This will help them recognize words and letters later on.

As children grow, read longer picture books. Ask them to describe what's going on in the pictures and to retell the stories you've read to them. Sometimes children want to hear one book over and over. This is tough on the reader, but rehearing a favorite story can fill important emotional needs. It also provides language practice that's as important to a child as practicing a concerto is for a musician.

Set the example of reading. Even young children recognize its importance when they see their parents reading and when books, magazines, and newspapers are familiar objects at home.

Independent reading

As children begin work on recognizing letters and words, and later, reading sentences and stories, be encouraging and enthusiastic. But don't push; each child learns to read at a different speed and over a long period of time. If your child is feeling frustrated, remind him or her of how much progress has been made.

Every day, set aside time for your child to read independently. The more practice children have at reading, the better they will get.

Continue to read aloud to your child as well. Children will stretch themselves to understand books that are too difficult for them to master on their own.

Make books available in your home; make sure your children get to the library; choose books for presents.

Talk to your children about the books they read independently. Doing this will help you keep in touch with their thoughts and concerns, even when they are older.

Helping your child learn to read is a responsibility, but it's fun, too. Forget the dishes and the lawn for fifteen minutes and sit down together with a good book. Reading with your children will give you some of the most treasured moments you will ever share.